To Queen Nily
D. J. S.

For Izzy and Jo
R. N.

BEACH LANE BOOKS • An imprint of Simon & Schuster Children's Publishing Division • 1230 Avenue of the Americas, New York, New York 10020 • Text copyright © 2017 by D. J. Steinberg • Illustrations copyright © 2017 by Robert Neubecker • All rights reserved, including the right of reproduction in whole or in part in any form. • BEACH LANE BOOKS is a trademark of Simon & Schuster, Inc. • For information about special discounts for bulk purchases, please contact Simon & Schuster Special Sales at 1-866-506-1949 or business@simonandschuster.com. • The Simon & Schuster Speakers Bureau can bring authors to your live event. For more information or to book an event, contact the Simon & Schuster Speakers Bureau at 1-866-248-3049 or visit our website at www.simonspeakers.com. • Book design by Lauren Rille • The text for this book was set in ITC New Baskerville • Manufactured in China • 0417 SCP • First Edition • 10 9 8 7 6 5 4 3 2 1 • CIP data for this book is available from the Library of Congress. • ISBN 978-1-4814-2657-2 (hardcover) • ISBN 978-1-4814-2658-9 (eBook)

KING LOUIE'S SHOES

written by
D. J. Steinberg

illustrated by
Robert Neubecker

BEACH LANE BOOKS

New York   London   Toronto   Sydney   New Delhi

LOUIS THE FOURTEENTH was a very **big** king.

How **big** was he?

He was **so big** that . . .

He ruled France for 72 years.

He built the **biggest palace** in the world
in the town of Versailles.

He grew the **biggest army** in all of Europe.

He threw the **biggest parties** for his royal family and friends.

And he gave the **biggest gifts,** mostly paintings and statues of himself.

There was only one little problem. . . .

King Louis the Fourteenth
was **NOT** big.

King Louie (which is how you say "Louis" in French)
was a shrimp.

"Royal Carpenter!" called King Louie.
"Build me a throne **so high** that
everyone will know just how big I am."

So the Royal Carpenter did.

When King Louie climbed up on that throne,
he was the **tallest king in the world.**
But King Louie could not sit up there all day.
When he came down, he was still a shrimp.

"Royal Hairdresser!" called King Louie.
"Make me the **biggest wig** ever,
so that everyone will know just how big I am."

So the Royal Hairdresser did.

King Louie strutted the streets of Paris in his new do . . . .

until it rained.

The king looked down sadly,
and saw his feet. . . .

"Royal Shoemaker!" called King Louie. "Make me the **biggest shoes ever,** so that everyone will know just how big I am."

So the Royal Shoemaker did.

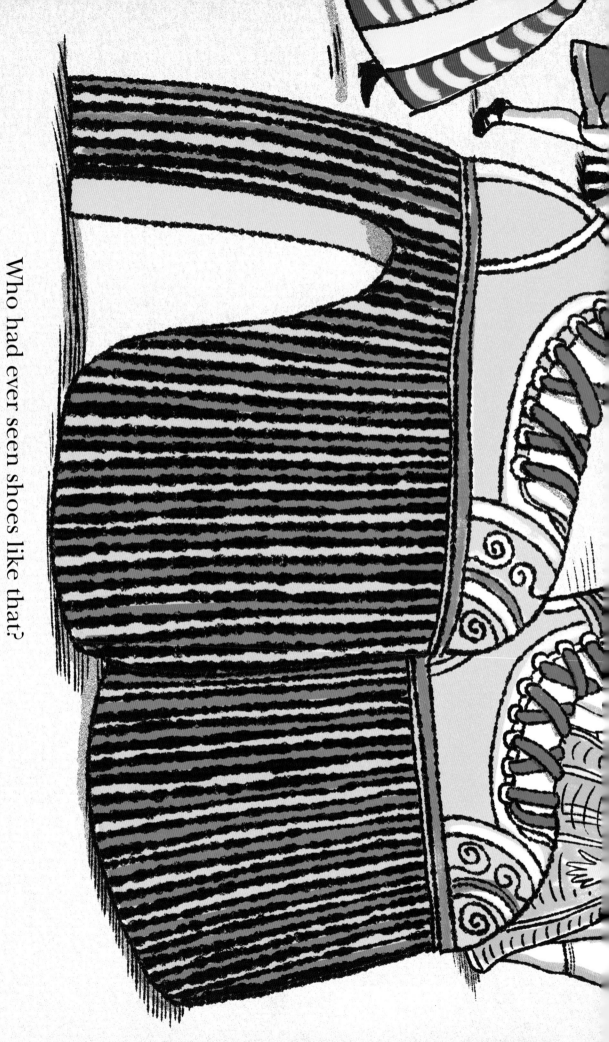

Who had ever seen shoes like that?
In the 1600s, heels were supposed to be flat!
King Louie's family and friends loved his new shoes.
They loved them so much . . .

The people *ooohed*

and *aaahed*

and *ooo-lah-lahed*.

they all got new shoes too!

That was a problem.

So King Louis the Fourteenth issued a decree:

NO ONE CAN WEAR SHOES TALLER THAN THE KING'S!

And to make extra sure,
he got a new pair of shoes.

How tall were the king's new shoes?

They were **so tall** that the king needed his servants to lift his feet in and out of the royal coach.

King Louie had to bend down to enter the big Baroque Ball without *ba*-reaking his royal head.

And when the king got up to lead the first dance . . .

he fell flat on his royal *derriere!*

(Which is French for, well, the part he fell on.)

King Louie did not feel
very big just then.

Now the people will laugh at me! he thought.
Now they will know!

But the people did not laugh.

They knew that because of the king, France was a proud and mighty nation. Thanks to King Louie, their lives were happy and safe.

So what if he was a shrimp?

The king looked around.
All the people bowed and cheered for him
to go on dancing.
But how could he, with those crazy shoes?

Off came the shoes.
Up came the king.

"**Hurrah!**" sang the crowd.

King Louis the Fourteenth must have felt
bigger than **big** that night,
with his family and friends all around,
as he spun and swayed to the music . . .

dancing holes in his stocking feet!

FOURTEEN FACTS ABOUT

1. **KINDERGARTEN KING!** Louis the Fourteenth was not even five years old when he was crowned the king of France in 1643.

2. **RECORD REIGN.** He reigned for seventy-two years. When he died in 1715, Louis had broken the record for longest ruler ever of a major European country.

3. **NICKNAME FAME.** The king was so powerful that people called him "Louis the Great" and the "Sun King" (but not "Shorty"!).

4. **VIVE LA FRANCE!** Louis made France the mightiest nation in Europe. He built an army of 400,000 soldiers and waged three major wars and many battles to keep the borders safe.

5. **MAIL-ORDER BRIDE?** War was not the only way to keep his foes away. Louis asked the daughter of his rival, the king of Spain, to marry him. Clever, *oui*?

6. **LOUIE-LAND!** The Palace of Versailles and its gardens were 87,729 square feet—that's the size of three Disneylands! (Filled with activities to keep his friends entertained, it was actually a lot like the Disneyland of its time.)

7. **SEEING DOUBLE?** Louis put 357 mirrors in the palace hall, so he always had a place to check if his wig was on straight! (The king owned more than 1,000 wigs.)

LOUIS THE FOURTEENTH

8. **LITTLE KING, BIG APPETITE!** Much of Louis's day was spent eating. That little king had a big stomach. No, really—after he died, doctors found out that his stomach was twice the size of an average man's!

9. **NOBLES, BEWARE!** Afraid that his nobles might plot against him, the king kept them close by and busy with many court ceremonies so he could watch them. He gave out honors, like tasting the king's dinner for him in case it was poisoned!

10. **LOUIE'S FAVORITE SUBJECT?** Himself, of course! Louis kept oodles of artists around to paint his portrait and war triumphs. He put up statues of himself throughout France.

11. **GOING FOR BAROQUE!** The dramatic, ornate style of art and music during the period of King Louis the Fourteenth is called "Baroque."

12. **DANCING KING.** Louis loved ballet and often went onstage to dance with the ballerinas. He liked to lead the first dance at his royal parties.

13. **HOW SHORT WAS HE?** In his bare feet, Louis was 5'4" short. But add five inches for his fancy heels and twenty feet for the throne he had built, and he towered 25'9" over his visitors when they came to see him!

14. **LOUIE'S LEGACY.** High-heeled shoes stayed popular with both men and women for over a hundred years after King Louis's time. Eventually, men went back to wearing shoes with regular heels, but for ladies, high heels are still in fashion to this very day.